This book is dedicated to our Creator.

We are a faith-based company striving to glorify God in all our affairs and firmly believe that good stewardship fosters positive results.

Susi B. Marketing, Inc.
"Because it's good for you!"

THIS BOOK BELONGS TO

_____

**Special thanks to our team of illustrators and graphic designers
who brought Angie and friends to life!
Book Design and Art Direction by CreativeBlox
Character Design, Pencils & Digital Color by Marcela Ribero
Inks by Gabriel Guzman**

**Published & Distributed by Susi B Marketing, Inc.
For More Information**
www.AngieTheAnt.com

Angie the Ant and The Bumblebee Tree©
© 2005 Susi B. Marketing, Inc.
Written by Susi Beatty and Keri Gunter

Summary: Headstrong yet compassionate, a young ant escapes captivity in a quest to liberate her people from the tyrannical rule of Sadina, queen of the evil Fleavils.

ISBN 0-9773653-0-1

Angie the Ant
and The Bumblebee Tree

By Susi Beatty and Keri Gunter

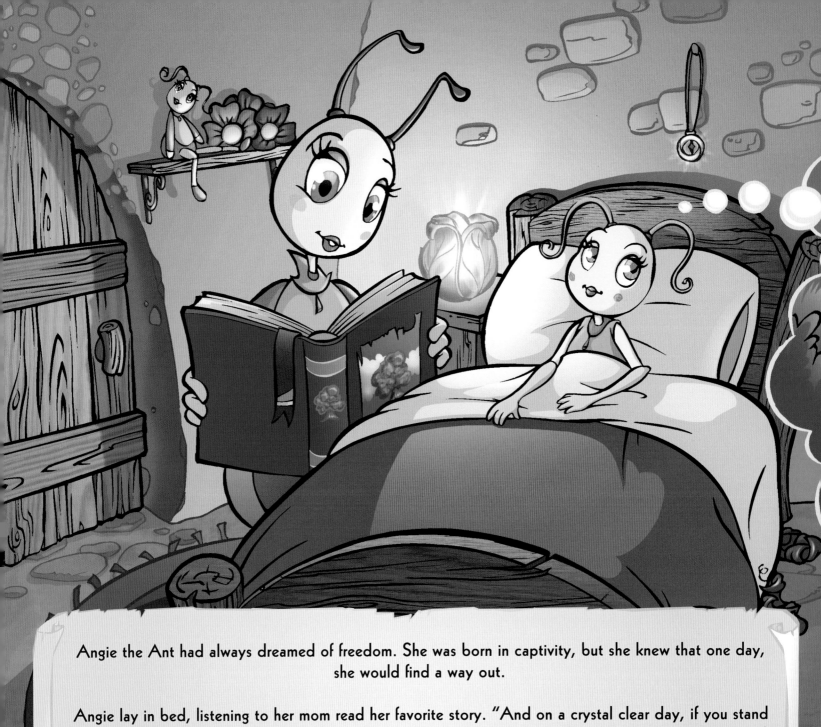

Angie the Ant had always dreamed of freedom. She was born in captivity, but she knew that one day, she would find a way out.

Angie lay in bed, listening to her mom read her favorite story. "And on a crystal clear day, if you stand on the highest peak, you just **might** be able to see the Bumblebee Tree. Older than time and sustained by the love of life," her mom continued, "the Bumblebee Tree is a gateway of safe passage to the Land of Antamar, where freedom reigns for all."

Angie interrupted. "So, if we can make it to the Bumblebee Tree, we'll be free like everyone in the Land of Antamar. Right, Mom?" Angie asked. "One day, we'll make it there. I just know it."
"Sweet little Angie! You're always getting your hopes up," her mom said. "Now, go to sleep. It's late."
"Okay," said Angie with a sigh. "Goodnight Mom."
Angie lived with her mother in Colony Pointe, a small village enslaved by Sadina, Queen of the Fleavils. All her life, she had heard about the Bumblebee Tree. She longed to live in the peaceful realm of Antamar, which lay just beyond the tree's mighty trunk.

Angie lay awake in bed. She knew the time had finally come to escape.
"It's the only way that Mom and I will ever be free," she thought.
Reaching the Bumblebee Tree was something worth fighting for, despite the danger of being caught by the Fleavils. Angie was ready. She would leave at daybreak. She had recently been given her grandmother's lucky medallion, which had protected her family for centuries. The medallion almost guaranteed her safety! Angie reviewed her plan and fell asleep.

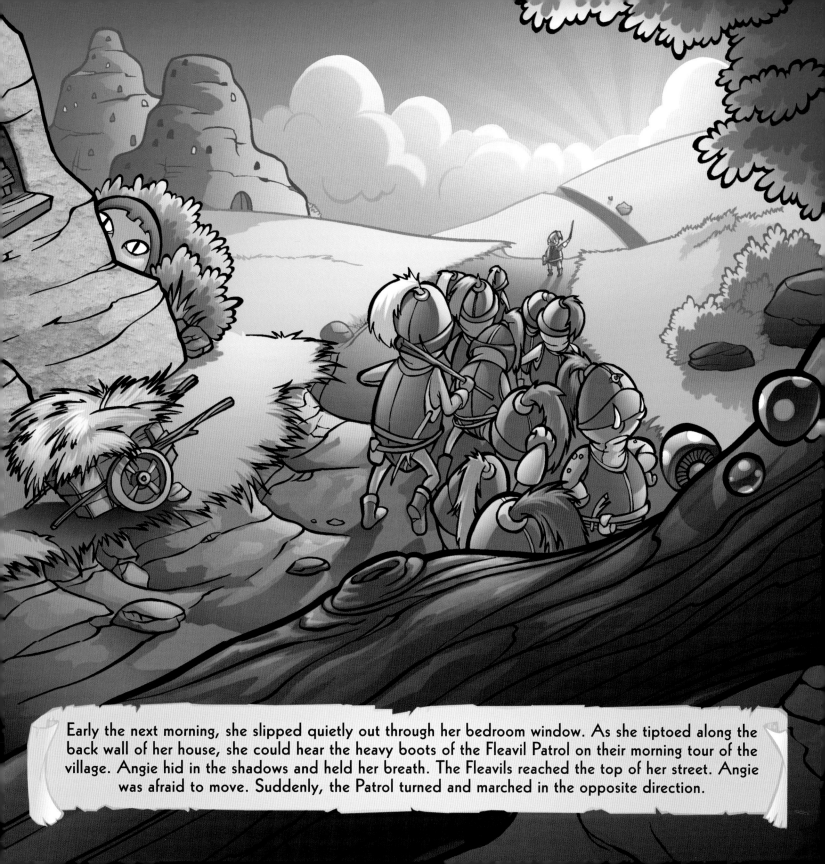

Early the next morning, she slipped quietly out through her bedroom window. As she tiptoed along the back wall of her house, she could hear the heavy boots of the Fleavil Patrol on their morning tour of the village. Angie hid in the shadows and held her breath. The Fleavils reached the top of her street. Angie was afraid to move. Suddenly, the Patrol turned and marched in the opposite direction.

With a sigh of relief, Angie made a break for it. The Fleavils didn't see the tiny figure as she disappeared into the trees. Secluded in the forest, she glanced back for a moment at the only home she had ever known.
"Somehow, some way," Angie thought,
"I'll make it to the Bumblebee Tree. Then, I'll come back to help my mom."

For now, she had to focus on her quest. First, her plan was to climb to the top of Colony Peak to see which way to go. She scrambled over rocky ledges, overgrown with vines and still slippery from the morning dew. Suddenly, she lost her footing and tumbled over the edge.
"Oh no!" she screamed. "Somebody, help me!" As Angie fell through the air, she tried to grab a twig to break her fall. **KATHUMP!** She landed on a fluffy pile of feathers and passed out.

On a sunny afternoon, Frankie the Blue Heron normally would have been out surfing,
but it was Angie's good luck that today, he had an urgent job to do.
As Angie started to wake up, she could hear Frankie singing,
**"Bumblebee Tree! Bumblebee Tree!
Where in the world is Bartlebee?"**

"Bartle-who?" Angie asked.
"Hey, little dudette! You're awake. I was getting worried. That was quite a fall."
"What happened? Where am I?" Angie asked, still groggy.
"Hold that thought, chica. I'm looking for a place to stop."

"Who are you?" asked Angie.
"I'm Frankie the Blue Heron, surfer dude extraordinaire! At your service Ma'am,"
said the big, goofy bird, nodding his head.
"My name is Angie," she replied.
"Nice to meet you, Angie," Frankie said. "I'm looking for Prince Bartlebee.
I have to take him back to the Bumblebee Tree. King's orders!"
Angie could hardly believe her good fortune. "The Bumblebee Tree? That's where I'm headed!" she said.

"I dunno, chica," Frankie said. "Things aren't so safe right now. The Fleavil armies are everywhere!"
"Believe me, I know all about Fleavils," Angie said. "I've been in Fleavil captivity all my life. I just escaped this morning, but it wasn't easy."
Frankie's eyes grew wide, and he flapped his wings. His new companion had suddenly impressed him.
"Escaped? I've never known anyone who escaped!"
With that, Angie couldn't turn back. She was officially on her way to the Bumblebee Tree.

Frankie and Angie flew over hills and valleys, across the desert and above rocky canyons.
They were looking for Bartlebee, but all the while, Angie kept an eye out for the Bumblebee Tree.
She wondered how far away it was and how long it would take to get there.
The world was much bigger than she ever imagined while growing up in Colony Pointe.

The blue heron and the young ant were careful to avoid the Fleavils.
The armies were marching everywhere. They flew over the beach on Surfsong Bay and saw
someone surfing on the waves. Frankie swooped down to take a closer look.

"Bartlebee! My little buddy bee!" shouted Frankie.
"Dude! What are you doing here?" Bartlebee yelled back.
"I'm here to save your little bumblebee neck again, pal. There's a whole army of Fleavils advancing this way!" Frankie said.
"Aw, man! I don't see anything!" Bartlebee said.
"Trust me, dude, they're coming. Jump up! Let's go!" Frankie insisted.
Bartlebee reluctantly jumped on Frankie's back, leaving his surfboard behind.

Angie moved over for Bartlebee. "I'm Angie," she said.
"It's too bad you couldn't bring your board."
"I'm Bartlebee," he replied, "but I guess you already know that." He turned and shouted in the big bird's ear. "What's up, Frankie? Do we really have to go? The waves, dude! Just look at them!"
At that moment, he saw his board wash up onshore, only to be torn to shreds by an army of Fleavils.
Frankie craned his neck around and raised his brow.
"Well?" he said.
The blue heron and the bumblebee nodded knowingly at each other, and the three friends were off.

They flew until dark and found a cave to rest in for the night.
Even though Fleavils despised rocky places, the travelers could feel Queen Sadina's presence all around.

Angie was excited and frightened at the same time. Too restless to sleep,
she reached into her pocket and held her lucky medallion for comfort.
She thought of her mom and missed her.
Soon, the brave, young ant drifted into dreams of the Bumblebee Tree and the freedom of Antamar.

The next morning, Angie was the first to awake.
Her stomach growled from hunger, so she crept out of the cave in search of food.
As she trekked through the woods, she stubbed her toe on something small and round. It flashed as it rolled in front of her. Angie had never seen anything like it.
The exterior was clear, and it had a ruby center. She studied the treasure for a moment and put it in her pocket for safekeeping. Soon, she came to an open field full of berries and forgot about her discovery.

"Angie!" she heard Bartlebee shouting from the sky.
"We were worried about you!" The Prince waved as Frankie pulled in for the landing.
"Yeah, chica. You really shouldn't wander off like that," Frankie said.
"I know. I'm sorry," said Angie, "but look at what I found for breakfast!"
"Wow! Way to go!" said Bartlebee.
He and Frankie dove into the berries, and the three friends ate their fill.
They loaded up for later and took off, heading north.
Surely, today they would reach the Bumblebee Tree.

They flew all day. As the sun was setting,
Angie saw something beautiful shining on the horizon.
"Bartlebee, is that ...?" Angie asked.
"Yes, Angie. That's the Bumblebee Tree. It always glows just before sunset," Bartlebee replied.

"Dude! Something's not right," Frankie said. Then, Bartlebee and Angie noticed a dark cloud surrounding the tree. "Fleavils!" Angie said under her breath.
"Let's head to the outpost," Bartlebee suggested.
"Maybe someone from the Bumblebee Tree Patrol is there."

When they reached the outpost, Doogie Dan, head of the BBT Patrol, greeted them.
"Prince Bartlebee, we're so grateful that you've returned. Good work, Frankie!"
"Thanks, man," Frankie replied. "This is our new friend, Angie."
"Welcome, Angie," Doogie Dan said. "I only wish our situation was better. The Bumblebee Tree is
surrounded by Fleavils, and we don't have a Weebie. Without a Weebie, we have no way to break
through the enemy lines. Plenty are scattered on the ground under the tree, but we can't reach them."
"What's a Weebie?" Angie asked.
"It's so awesome! It's crystal clear with a ruby center," Frankie replied.
"You mean like this?" Angie pulled the tiny treasure out of her pocket
and held it in the palm of her hand. Everyone gasped.

"Where did you get that?" Bartlebee asked.

"I found it this morning," Angie said.

"Indeed!" Doogie Dan said. "It appears that you've found a baby Weebie, though I don't quite understand how. I thought there was only one Bumblebee Tree."

"Will it help?" Angie asked.

"Of course it will!" Doogie Dan replied. "Baby Weebies are much more potent than mature ones. This is just what we need!"

Angie held the key to their success. The four friends stayed up all night, planning their attack.

At dawn, Angie, Bartlebee, Frankie and the BBT Patrol hid in the brush to the east of the tree. When the sun rose, Frankie stretched his wing back and took careful aim. With one precise motion, he flung the baby Weebie into the heart of the Fleavil encampment.

WEEEEEEEEEbieeeeeeee ... ka-TINK! POOF!

Fleavils scattered in every direction. They left a path just wide enough for Angie and Bartlebee to enter the Bumblebee Tree's field of protection.

Frankie shouted, "Cover me, Angie!"

He swooped towards them, followed by Doogie Dan and the BBT Patrol.

Soon, everyone had crossed to safety. They fought their best with the help of the Weebies and drove

away all the Fleavil forces.

"Hurrah! Hurrah!" Triumphant cheers resounded from inside the Bumblebee Tree.

Angie could hardly believe she was finally going to see...

Antamar! It was more glorious than she had ever imagined! Overlooking lush green fields and rolling hills, the Bumblebee Tree was the grand gateway to Antamar, the land of freedom. Professor Mopkins and Flumpy, two of the Bumblebee King's most trusted friends, greeted Bartlebee and his group.

"Ppprince Bbbartlebee!"
Flumpy stammered. "Wwwelcome home!"
"Thanks, Flumpy," Bartlebee said.
"You must be Angie," said Professor Mopkins.
"How did you know?" Angie asked.
"Since the invasion, we've been in constant contact with the outpost," Mopkins said.
"The King is anxious to see you all."

They entered the grand hall of the castle, where the Bumblebee King himself
was waiting to greet them.
"Welcome home, my son," said King Bradford as he embraced Prince Bartlebee.
"And welcome back, Frankie. Good job!"
Frankie took a bow. "I couldn't have done it without Angie," he replied.
"Yes, I've heard," the King answered. He turned to Angie. "So you're the one who found the baby
Weebie and saved the Bumblebee Tree! We are forever grateful to you."
"Thanks," Angie said, smiling proudly.
"I would do anything to help protect the Bumblebee Tree and Antamar."

"I'm glad to hear it," the King said, "because we will need your help again. Undoubtedly, the Weebie you found came from a Bumblebee Tree seedling. If the seedling grows into a tree, it could become another gateway to Antamar.
Will you help us find the seedling before Queen Sadina does?"Angie's goal had been to find the Bumblebee Tree so she could lead her people to freedom. But she knew that if the Fleavils took over Antamar, there would be no hope for anyone.
"Of course I'll help," she said.
"Excellent!" the King replied. "Now, let the feasting and celebration begin!"
Everyone knew there would be great danger and adversity in the adventures that lay ahead. But working together, Angie and her friends would surely triumph
for the freedom of Antamar. This was just the beginning.

To be continued...

ABOUT THE AUTHORS

Susi Beatty has a diverse background spanning from international recording artist and professional songwriter to US Karate Federation team member.
Susi is an entrepreneur with a business degree from the College of Charleston and has an MA in Clinical Counseling from Webster University. Susi believes that serving others is the key to happy living. In 2005, she founded Susi B. Marketing, Inc. with the goal of launching an icon that will be the national mascot for child abuse prevention.
She currently resides in Charleston, SC with her two labs, Summer and Sunshine.

Keri Gunter graduated from BYU-Hawaii with a BA in English and theater. She has a diverse background in both the corporate and non-profit worlds, specializing in marketing and communications. Keri is thrilled for the opportunity to be writing again, especially with the intention of making a positive impact on the world. She grew up in South Carolina and is happy to call Charleston her home.